SPRING

AN ALPHABET ACROSTIC

SPRING

AN ALPHABET ACROSTIC

by Steven Schnur
Illustrated by Leslie Evans

CLARION BOOKS

New York

Clarion Books
a Houghton Mifflin Company imprint
215 Park Avenue South, New York, NY 10003
Text copyright © 1999 by Steven Schnur
Illustrations copyright © 1999 by Leslie Evans

Illustrations executed in hand-colored linoleum cut blocks.
Text is 19/25-point Galliard.
Art direction and book design by Carol Goldenberg.
Printed in Singapore.

Library of Congress Cataloging-in-Publication Data
Schnur, Steven.
Spring: an alphabet acrostic / by Steven Schnur ; illustrated by Leslie Evans.
p.   cm.
Summary: Describes spring, with its animals, green smells, and renewed outside activities.
When read vertically, the first letters of the lines of text spell related words arranged alphabetically,
from "April" to "zenith."
ISBN 0-395-82269-6
1. Spring—Juvenile literature. 2. Acrostics—Juvenile literature. [1. Spring. 2. Acrostics. 3. Alphabet.]
I. Evans, Leslie, ill. II. Title.
QB637.7.S29   1998 Suppl.
793.73[E]—dc21   98-22704
CIP   AC

TWP 10 9 8 7 6 5 4 3 2 1

For Mom, ever Allegre

—S.S.

To my sisters, Kim, Pam, and Beth

—L.E.

After days of
Pouring
Rain, the last
Ice and snow finally
Leave the earth.

Beyond our
Upstairs window
Dead-looking branches
Suddenly spring to life.

Cows, heavy with milk, loll
Among their newborns
Licking them as they
Feed.

Day breaks early now
And quickly
Warms after a cool
Night.

Egrets, ducks, and **G**eese nest in the marsh **G**rass, waiting for their **S**hells to hatch.

From the mud
Ringing the
Old cow pond come
Grunts, whistles, and croaks.

Green leaves overhead, a
Rug of green underfoot,
And the air between
Sweet with the green
Smell of spring.

Hair swaying, each girl leaps
On one foot
Past the first
Space,
Crouches and springs
Once, twice, three
Times, returns and
Collects her marker, then jumps
Home.

In the nursery a
New baby sleeps while
Family
And
Neighbors gather
To celebrate.

Jammed between an
Unpainted fence and the
Neighbor's
Garage, old
Lumber, tangled vines, and
Evergreen saplings.

Knees pumping, we run
Into the wind, strings
Taut,
Eyes fixed on the
Sky.

Leaning
Against the house,
Dad, covered with
Dust and paint from
Ear to ear, climbs to the next
Rung.

Mild days,
Apple blossoms, and
Yellow daffodils.

Nestled under the
Eaves, a
Song-filled ark of
Twigs and grass.

On a hill
Under flowering
Trees, we
Sit
In the shade
Dreaming and
Eating berries.

Parents, children,
And a
Row of drummers march
Alongside a
Dazzling red fire
Engine.

Quick, count
Up the new kittens: one
In a box
Near the furnace,
Twins
Under the
Porch, a
Little white-
Eared one on the stairs, and
This calico
Sleeper in the laundry basket.

Rounding
A bend, we
Float downstream on logs
Tied tightly together.

Sown in freshly plowed
Earth, they grow
Each
Day a little nearer the
Sun.

Under a rising
Moon, two teams
Play ball
In a dusky field
Ringed by
Early corn.

Visible in the
Eastern sky,
Now that summer is nearly
Upon us, the morning
Star.

White June
Heat begins to ripen
Each green
And
Trembling stalk.

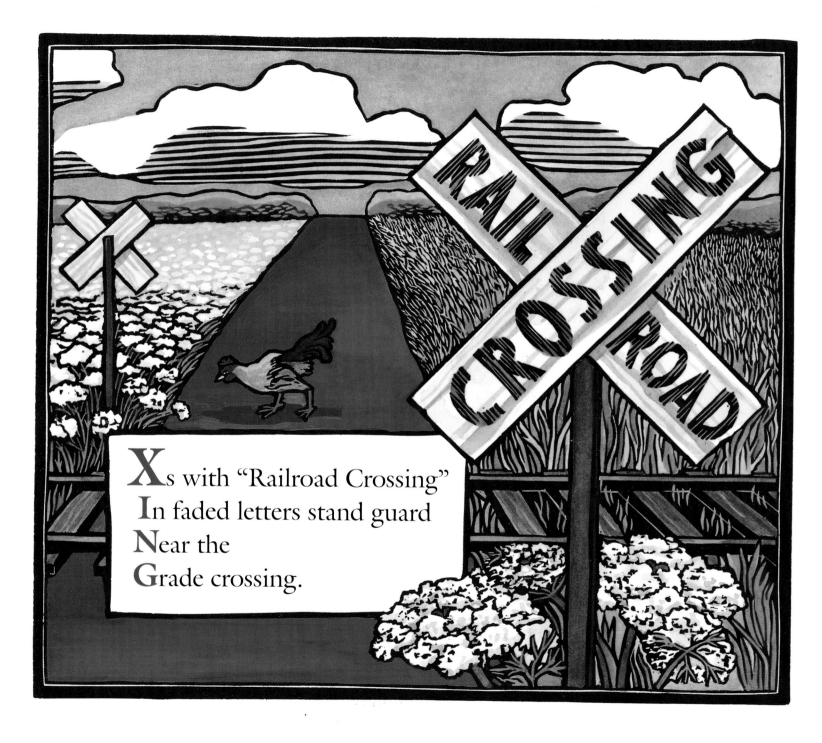

Xs with "Railroad Crossing"
In faded letters stand guard
Near the
Grade crossing.

Yellow goslings turning brown,
One lamb joins the flock,
Up in the oak
Nests emptying, all the newborns
Growing.

Zucchinis and
Eggplants are greening
Now that summer
Is finally here and
The hot sun is
High overhead.